ROBERT FERGUSON

LOVE YOU, World!

novum pro

All rights of distribution, including via film, radio, and television, photomechanical reproduction, audio storage media, electronic data storage media, and the reprinting of portions of text, are reserved.

Printed in the European Union on environmentally friendly, chlorine- and acid-free paper.

© 2025 novum publishing gmbh
Rathausgasse 73, A-7311 Neckenmarkt
office@novum-publishing.co.uk

ISBN 978-3-7116-0469-9
Editing: Chris Beale
Cover photo:
Rangizzz | Dreamstime.com
Cover design, layout & typesetting:
novum publishing

www.novum-publishing.co.uk

Acknowledgements

"The Cosmic Search" and "Almost" were first published in "The Cannon's Mouth", the quarterly anthology of Cannon Poets.

Huge thanks are due to all the Cannon Poets for their warm welcome and invaluable advice, to the members of Solihull Writers' Workshop, to Lydia Towsey and the members of Word!, and especially to Charlie Jordan for the inspiration repeatedly generated in their workshops.

All peculiarities of interpretation are my own.

Introduction

Being blessed with a long life, I have many memories, most of them dim until stimulated by companions' talk, and a lot of them shared by other people walking the same long road. For me, the memories seem to return most easily in verse, and the clearest of them relate to the most important aspects of an active life.

This collection therefore includes more poems about love – could we exist fully without it? – the childhood in which we were formed, some stupid risks and lucky escapes from before we knew better, critical issues (climate change and interpersonal tolerance get a mention), the inevitability of ageing and its limitations, animals (especially cats, of course) who accompany us and teach us so many truths, and a nod towards humour, without which, however peculiar, it would sometimes seem difficult to go on. There is no particular theme, just the reflections of a life thoroughly enjoyed, set down to spark the readers' own memories and enjoyment.

Robert Ferguson
Spring, 2024

Index of Titles

Apple Green	13
The Kitchen Range	14
Early Lesson	15
Coin	16
Across Vauxhall Bridge	17
Sporting Preference	18
At The Fold In The Map	19
Somelier	20
Almost	21
Broken Isolation	22
Holding Hands	23
Caress	24
A Feather	25
A Doorway In Granada	26
Bear Kindness	28
A Thousand Tiny Collisions	29
Letter From Love	30
Reply To Love's Letter	31
Return	32
Autumn Of Love	34
Pedantry	35
I Am	36
Layers	37
Changes	38
Autumn	39
October	40
Friday	41
Flying A Glider	42
Season's End, Hastings	43
Survival	44
Snow Gulley	45
Dignity	46

An Unsure Hand	47
Disabled Visitors	48
Two Couples	49
Invocation	50
What Would I Do Without You?	51
The Last Five Years	52
The Table	54
Boxfiles	55
Salvation	56
Let It Go	57
The Cosmic Search	58
Ouroboros	59
Hallowe'en	60
Violets	61
The Wonder Of The Moon	62
Visiting The Moon	63
Interrupting Jane Austen's Maid	64
A Bit Of Bad Luck	65
Angels	66
Prayer	68
Chime	69
Prejudice	70
The Ivory Bangle Lady	71
Baroness Doreen Thomas	72
Alma Woodsey Thomas	73
Names And Heritage	74
Spring Planning	75
Lambs In Spring	76
Spring Cinquaine	77
Paris	78
Night Journey	79
Climate Change At Kandersteg	80
Kittiwakes	81
Family And Friends	82
Claw Wisdom	83
Communication	84

Curiosity	85
Why Do Cats Exist?	86
Bobbled	87
Introduction	88
Worker Bee	89
Euphoria I	90
Euphoria II	91
Red Leather Slippers	92
Disaster Barely Averted	93
Unavoidable Family Christmas	94
He Wasn't There Again Today	95
I Will Smile	96

Apple Green

The smell hits you as you climb the unsteady ladder
Into the house-wide loft. It's solid,
Nothing like the smell when they hanged in the orchard.
Much stronger. Not the rot-smell of fallen fruit,
Wasp-drilled as if to be screwed back
Onto the tree. No, these green globes have been dressed
Each in its own square suit of torn paper
And laid in its place on the planks
Stretching between the roof-tile battens
On either side. The smell has a colour,
Apple green, which deepens with the early frosts
Until most of the fruit have been chosen,
Transported in round wicker baskets to the kitchen,
And cored and cooked in sauces and pies for Christmas.

The Kitchen Range

Set into the wall, and forbidden
For safety, but still the centre
Of life for the family, whose chairs,
Each jealously allocated,
Are gathered round it
After meals. "Five minutes for the Queen."
Aside, the scuttle from which Mother throws,
And Father places, reflective coal
On the dull embers behind sooty bars.
The baking oven's heavy iron door
Is never opened. Bread is bought
And Grandma slices it
In wafers, and then spreads
The raspberry jam, boiled there
In a copper cauldron,
Stood there on the hob to cool,
Bottled on the table unchenilled
For the purpose,
Spills rubbed into the carpet
Where I play.

Early Lesson

I sat at the end on the left,
Looked at by the big boy at the end of the table.
I was small, the smallest,
From whom nothing was expected but silence and a clean plate
Whatever was served that day.
So I learned to eat everything –
Grey mutton, thin gravy, lumpy mash,
Boiled and boiled and boiled cabbage –
And it served me well.
When abroad in different cultures,
When offered hospitality by non-culinary friends,
In cheap cafes, presumptuous banquets,
I always manage to present
A clean plate.

Coin

If I were a coin
I'd be tempted to be a penny.
Not a modern one, insignificant
In size and colour.
One from my boyhood, an inch across
That, when you had a few,
You could clink them together in your pocket
To show you were rich,
Or at least had enough for a 'phone call.

No, not even one of those.
Rather, something silver.
A Half-a-Crown, like those a barely-known rich uncle
Left on his occasional visits?
Untold wealth! "Put it in your money box."
"Yes, Ma." – reluctantly.

No, that's too big and flashy.
What I'd like to be is a Silver Joey.
Not worth a lot, but enough
For an ice cream in those days.
A bit of pleasure for a tiny gleam.

Across Vauxhall Bridge

Red Routemasters clustered in Camberwell Green
When we were young. Perhaps they still do,
But not as they were then
With an open rear platform for boarding
As they pulled away, and for leaving them
Between stops when the traffic delayed us
So that it was worth dropping off and dodging the cars,
Ignoring the "Oi!" from the Cheeky Clippy
Who'd seen us in the mirror at the bend in the stairs.

We went everywhere in those buses.
Few mates had cars, or were going
Where we wanted to go – Peckham Rye, New Cross or Dulwich,
Up the Palace or Catford Dog Track,
That pub stuck out over the river at Deptford
Or bounced on the humpbacked canal bridge
On the Old Kent Road, going up West.
We was the boys from Sauf o' the River.
No taxis came here, and we couldn't
Have afforded them if they had.
For us, it was always the Routemasters
Out of Camberwell Green.

Sporting Preference

Tennis in the park on a hot Wednesday.
Should be cricket, but none of us like that.
Delicate negotiations with the second Games master.
"Tell no one, and I'll overlook your absence.
Bring me tomorrow the ticket for hiring the court."
We probably sweated far more than third man or square leg
And had nothing to compare with George's brother's
Daisy chain from the long-on boundary.
A musician, a poet, a physicist and a linguist.
Creative types. Not the most popular.
I wonder what they got up to?
Where are they now?

At The Fold In The Map

One way, we cycled into the hard East wind
But over flat roads, giddy
Along embankments above fen drains,
Fearful of falling in.
The other way, the road went up and down
On the low, steep ironstone hills.
We got as tired on the one as the other,
Turning into the outgoing wind
To rest on the journey home.

Somelier

"What shall we drink with this, everybody?
I think a burgundy with the beef,
And an Alsace with the fish before.
Have you got that, boy?"

"Yes, of course I want to taste it.
Of course we'll need a bucket.
Oh, it's already too warm to have a taste.
Take it back. No, we won't wait.
Bring us another bottle.
You can leave that one until it cools down."

"Uncork the Burgundy now, so it can breathe.
What? This is frozen. Get another.
Room temperature, boy. Where on earth do you keep it?"

But the chef put it in the bain-marie for me
And the old man never guessed.

Almost

Oh, the temptation! She sat low in the water.
Leaking? Sprung planks? No varnish
Where sun and salt had burned her paintwork.
White topsides blistered, needed scrubbing down to wood,
But long slim spars and mast speaking
Of power under a new suit of sails,
And brand new cordage throughout.
A snip of a price! "But likely to cost a fortune
To refurbish. And then there's a mooring.
And how often would you get down here?
For how long? You never have time to take a weekend off.
What if you got stuck by the tides,
Or no wind, or a sandbank?"
So he didn't buy the boat. But, oh, the temptation!

Broken Isolation

Clamour can be so demanding
When one longs for peace
Without additional involvements.

No sight of the way forward.
Nothing to be done.
It must sort itself out.

Despair.

And then you message me, send photos,
Cats, goslings, dawn, hills, books.

Immediately I am cheered.
I smile without intention.
You are here in absence.

This is why you exist
And you are hugely treasured in my world.

Holding Hands

In the dark, our hands touched
By accident, truly,
Opened, and closed around each other,
And held.
So long since it happened.
Such release, such sudden fire
Of acceptance, such happiness,
And our hands held together,
Even after the lights went up.

Caress

Among the demanding icons on my desktop,
Between the urgent texts, the detailed emails,
Your voice, released by a tap on the arrowhead,
Your loving care, tracking narrower and wider
Along the call.
Checking, encouraging, from far away
But warm enough to be here beside me.
I feel your hand holding mine.

A Feather

Long, dun, soft as silk,
The partridge lost it from her wing this morning,
Dropped like a courtly lady's handkerchief
In the path of her beloved. I do hope
She doesn't miss it terribly, and fly unbalanced.
I shall give it another use,
Perhaps as a quill. I'll sharpen the end with a razor blade
And slit it to let the ink flow evenly
Across the page of my letter to my love.

A Doorway In Granada

In the cobbled street across the valley
From the huge sprawling castle
Dim in the grey-blue clouds
Nearly a mile away, but haunting,

There is a whitewashed house, with pantiles
Extended over a spreading balcony
Wide enough to drink coffee with breakfast
Or wine with luxurious dinners among friends
In the warm tangible darkness of a summer night.

Below the veranda, on street-level,
Is a door, arch-topped and tiny
To keep out the day's heat
And the early morning's chill.

Push this door gently. It will swing open,
Leading to a dark kitchen filled with smells
Of pot-grown fresh herbs
Bubbling in huge smoke-stained saucepans,
Meat and fish from the oven below.

Another door leads (duck your head)
To the peace of a garden,
Where gravelled paths wander
Between Alibaba pots stuffed full of flowers.

Vines grow up the walls, blossoms tumble
In window-boxed tumult.
I would take you to live here for ever,
If only I dared.

Bear Kindness

A black bear came through my kitchen door.
Torrential rain had sleeked her fur to nylon.
Blinded, she took off her glasses so she could see,
Then her bonnet, and shook her hair out
Over the newspaper spread on my table.
Unbuttoned her head-to-toe raincoat, peeled it off
And at last I could see who was there.
She bent to her sturdy boots, threw them into a corner
And pushed off her waterproof leggings
As I rose to reach for the mop.
At last I could hug the damp human
Who had braved an unprecedented downpour
In her kindness, to cross the city
And make sure that I was all right.

A Thousand Tiny Collisions

Atoms buzz silently in my bloodstream,
Heating my skin in their excitement,
Banging together in the stress of my earnest hope
That you will actually come to meet me,
Recognise me from my halting description,
Discount the self-doubt I tried to hide on the telephone,
Give way to curiosity at least
Within the mutual interests I detected
From our friend's laughing introduction.

I was early at our rendezvous.
Expect you will be just a little late,
Having paused on the nearest corner
To reconnaissance this halting person
With whom you agreed, now rashly-seeming,
To fill an otherwise empty afternoon.

Tension. Will you come?

Letter From Love

Dear ...

It's been a long time. Have you forgotten
How once you lived confidently in my company?
Kisses were frequent, first stolen then
Brashly taken, prolonged, extended almost for ever.
Hugs comforted and strengthened you when life opposed.
It's been a long time, though. Have you forgotten?
You might still be accepted, even though
Cuddles have become more painful,
Holding someone hurts and squeaks of anguish
Embarrass as they strike.
That's not for you to judge, dear.
I'd like to visit you again. You seem reluctant
To let me in, though I'm sure you're not.
Does this reluctance mark the intensity of your hope?
Try again, dear. And again, if necessary.
Open the door. Perhaps I'm waiting for you
Just the other side.

Reply To Love's Letter

Dear Love.

Yes, it has been ages since I felt your presence,
But it is most apt that your letter should arrive
Now. I have indeed met someone special,
Someone who has been infinitely kind to me,
Beautiful and fascinating beyond compare,
Shares my most ardent interests,
Patient beyond limit of my tentative cowardice.
Though I love her dearly,
And she lightens my life infinitely,
And, despite your reassurances,
And every other excuse my mind presents
(And they are many),
I shall not risk the love she gives me now
By telling her the full depth of my feelings.

But thank you for remembering me, nonetheless.

Return

Heavy air, thick, too difficult to breathe
Through the nose alone.
Not unpleasant, just over-warm
And dust-heavy.
Too many days away, avoiding memories,
But now, with courage gathered,
Without alternatives, she has come back.
Open a window, more.
Even that draught seems to be defeated
By the texture of the air, the memories.
He was here. They were here together.
She has moved his chair from the table
To the wall, just to change the pattern.
She puts his beaker into the bin.
He wouldn't drink, even ambrosia, from it
Any more, and she could not,
Even in his memory, in gratitude.
She takes a tealight and four scented squares of wax,
Lights the ceramic burner, adding to the air
Something different, to encourage the dilution.

Tomorrow, in air circulated, freshened, through the night,
She'll do more, sift the bookshelves,
Bag his pants and socks, and sort his jackets
For the charity shops in a nearby town,
But not too near, to avoid the embarrassment
Of hugging a well-known jacket from the back
Which turned out no longer to contain him.

Lying down, lost in the centre of a no-longer shared bed,
She didn't sleep.

Autumn Of Love

Not in your face, your lips, your eyes,
But in your reluctant hand,
Your withdrawn hip,
Something about your choice of words,
The loss of eye-contact over your fashionable tea,
I felt the freshness of the Autumn air,
The coming of Winter's chill.

Pedantry

I am
comfortable with words, better writing them than speaking
uncomfortable without the chance to choose them carefully
so that the unique meaning of each one is chosen specifically
to express what I want to describe or explain once
without ambiguity
there's a word for this that nobody says to me
I know it but have successfully ignored it for years.

I Am

exhausted by trying to do more than my body approves of
it's a habit with a background of Pavlovian guilt
when I rest and refuse to get on
with an expanding to-do list
learn
it will all get done eventually
perhaps not in the order you intended
and the world won't stop turning
even when others would prefer you to wear yourself out.

Layers

Nothing stands still, even when
You sit and watch the world go giddily round you
Leaving succeeding influences on each other
In layers that repeatedly change what was laid before,
And you see you were wrong, and admit it,
And move on.

Only an arrogant fool is not wrong, not ever.
No principle can withstand new knowledge, a new experience.
Conclusions must grow like flowerbeds,
Shoots poke through the earth, leaves rise, buds fill
And flower and die, give way to others,
And the whole bed changes
And no one and nothing ever, ever stands still.

Changes

Not everything changes, over however long.
Maybe from inside the womb, or shortly after,
Was I organised – cry, bottle, sleep,
Each in its proper place, so that
Now my books stand in sections of subjects
On bookshelves, my clothes have their drawers,
My CDs align by composer and K-number.
I've always done it, as long as I can remember.
Not everything changes, over however long.

Autumn

Now it's September. Everyone has gone home
And taken their families back from the tourist traps
To school and the office, and the prospect of Christmas to come.
I will be able to get a seat on a train
And a hotel room, and a table outside a café
With attentive service before it gets cold.
So it's time to come into the world again,
To explore and travel, and perhaps go wild.

October

Always so much to remember.
Planning the route of my next walk
Is part of shopping, so as to save time,
To be efficient,
But October is not an efficient time of the year.
Everything is slowing, being put away for the winter
Or being dragged out reluctantly
From where we put it busily and efficiently in the Spring.
Doing less means doing even less.
I want to stop being efficient completely.
Just sit for the last time on the garden bench
And let the world in my mind wander gently
Uncontrolled,
Or even stop.

Friday

Friday, I leave it all behind,
Catch a train, a flight,
Heave the golf clubs up onto my back,
My ropes and boots into the trunk of the car,
And go off to a totally different gang
With different jokes and different priorities.
Another part of me, unknown to those
Who share my week. Not necessarily more important,
Just different, just as dear and essential to me.

Flying A Glider

Flying a glider isn't difficult.
There's a technique for taking off, stick forward gently,
then hard back,
That's almost impossible to get wrong.
Once you are airborne and clear of everyone else,
Keep the nose level and turn, hands and feet together,
In pursuit of supportive thermals.
All this is easy enough.
The difficult bit is landing in one piece.
Don't get too far from a flat green field.
Don't give away too much height too early, or too late.
Don't bounce the skid off the aircraft.
Don't…

Aaah, we're down.

Season's End, Hastings

There have been two Autumn storms already
And I'm a fair-weather sailor,
So the dinghy and sails are in the rented store.
The mast and jibboom unstepped and laid aside
For re-varnishing, the standing tackle unrigged
Until next Spring. The hull is out of the water,
Hauled up on the shingle beach and careened,
And I'm scraping it. Almost a mindless occupation,
So the mind goes wandering, planning
For next year's voyages.

Survival

From the bow, watching the ice wall approach,
Would we survive for three months
With a boat, two tents and freeze-dried rations?
So much gear we didn't need.
Soap. Mountaineering boots – we lived in Wellingtons,
Even sleeping. On the two-thousand-foot cliff
Above the fjord, sun glaring off the glacier below,
The ice axe comforted, saved, as it did
Among the crevasses where we roped together,
And when the boat grounded, and on the volcano's slope.
We did survive. We learned that you survive or die.
Everything between is just a happy bonus for that day.

Snow Gulley

Space beneath my feet. It should be snow.
It was for the others. It gave way for me.
I'm sliding. Two thousand feet below
The fjord shines blue, reflecting a sun-filled sky.
I begin to feel fear. I mustn't tumble
But I do. My foot catches, head comes forward,
And now I'm somersaulting. Here comes death.
My rucksack's weight increases the rate of swing
But my ice axe is strapped to my right wrist.
I tuck its head under my armpit.
The point scrapes shallow snow off crumbling rock
And then digs in. Grasp the shaft with both hands.
Push hard. It's working. I'm no longer tumbling.
I stop, exhausted, my emptied rucksack slack upon my back.
I should be dead. Now just to climb back
Three hundred feet to where the others stand on solid rock,
Silent.

Dignity

Returning from the helpful optometrist
With my new glasses (not putting them on yet,
That would be giving up),
I stubbed the welt of my shoe on the pavement's edge,
And was only saved from falling by the strong, tactful hand
Of a young man, upright, forties,
(Younger than me, at least), who smiled non-condescendingly
Just to reassure me that added age
Hadn't yet removed all my dignity.

An Unsure Hand

The light in here isn't good.
Never noticed that before. Humph!
Makes my face look a bit like
The gentle hills of the North Downs.
Why should that be? Extra shadows
Where my cheeks and chin stick out.
Oh dear, it's bristles! But I shaved this morning.
Well, I pushed the razor over my soapy face.
It's a fairly new blade. Only a fortnight old.
Nothing lasts these days! Perhaps
I should try a new shaving soap?
Saw one on tele last night. Could have it by tomorrow,
But what a waste of half a tube of the old one.
And, anyway, what does it matter at my age?
Nobody's wanted to kiss me for years and years.

Disabled Visitors

"Let's visit the Castle", everyone said
And rushed off. I sat in my chair.
A mild-looking man stood by me
Gazing after them. "What did he say?" he asked.
"They're off to visit the Castle," I said.
"I'm sorry," the man replied. "What did he say?"
I pointed up the path. "Oh, the Castle,"
He said. "Would you like to see it?"
I nodded, pointed to my wheelchair, and smiled
Ruefully. "That's no problem," he said,
And took the handles, pushed me up the slope,
And together we had a really lovely day.

Two Couples

The stick was hanging on the arm of the bench
Beside the path. We sat down, and Stella unscrewed the flask.
"They won't have got far without that," she said.
I undid the sandwiches. "They'll be back for it
As soon as they miss it. It's probably only needed
For comfort rather than support."
"But feeling secure's important
Too," Stella said, sipping iced tea through a straw.
And, lo and behold, next minute, along the path,
Came a couple, the woman supporting the older man's arm.
"Oh, good", said the man, "You've found it.
We were talking, and
I just forgot it until we got to the muddy bit
Half a mile onwards." They sat down, took a sip of tea,
And shortly we all started off up the path again.

Invocation

In the darkness underneath the bed
I stretch my dust-flecked arm
Blindly, and find nothing.
It *must* be here!
Come on, St. Anthony! I really need your sight
And skill. It's my last painkiller.
I'll be in agony by morning
Without it.
Stretch again.
Ah! Heartfelt thanks, as fingers push then clasp
On the tiny tablet.
Well done, Anthony!

What Would I Do Without You?

First thing in a morning, once I've been washed and dressed
Like the baby I was almost eighty years ago,
Freedom returns, and I'm put in my wheelchair
And left alone to attack the world.

My prognosis suggests that, someday soon,
I shall be confined to my bed. Then I'll need
To re-arrange the furniture, get the laptop located
Somewhere handy, and the radio and tele and phone.

Just for now, though, the world is within reach each day,
Oh, wheelchair, what would I do without you?

The Last Five Years

Ten years ago, there were two of us.
Then there was only one, and
When I'd recovered, five years ago,
It was time to break out and play.
Four years ago, when I could still walk,
I explored Edinburgh and Dundee, and wrote a book
And went to the first gig ever in my life,
"Streisand in the Park."
Three years ago, being able to walk less,
But able to stand without pain,
I talked five friends into joining me
On a barge for a week.
They sunned themselves on the foredeck
And tended to the locks,
While I navigated the bends and bridges.
Later that year, I hired a personal tutor
To teach me enough Spanish to talk to waiters
And taxi drivers and policemen,
To hire a mobility scooter and have a Turkish bath
During three weeks in Granada.

Two years ago, I fell over repeatedly,
Confined myself to a wheelchair, but still enjoyed
The city-centre restaurants and theatres of my new home
And wrote more books of poetry.
Where will I be in five years' time? Perhaps not here at all,
But I am so thankful for the last five years.

The Table

I do have a table, with a generous surface area
But I've cluttered it with the keyboard
I never learned to play. I could put it back in its box
In the hall cupboard, free up the tabletop
And doubtless cover it with books and my big atlas,
Which would be quite useful, but that would be to accept defeat.
Should I try once again to bludgeon my arthritic fingers
And ageing brain to make sense of quavers and chords,
Or just accept that this is another thing
I shan't ever learn to do, like woodwork
And painting and cooking?

Boxfiles

Why did I choose the red boxfiles
For the papers, the flood of papers,
Arising from that Committee?
It's only been running a 12-month.
Now there are two bulging boxes,
Both of which have to be taken
To every meeting. In between meetings,
The files stare at me malevolently,
Demanding attention. They don't mean to bully.
It's just their aggressive colour – red, red, red!

Salvation

Whirling, whirling, whirling
I need to still my mind
It can't think, can't grasp more
I stand before the shelf on which the brass bowl sits
Touch it gently with its wooden spoon
The rich sound fills the air around my head
Quells the rushing. I sink to sit back straight on folded knees
Still, silenced, saved.

Let It Go

Let It go. You haven't been allowed in years to
Let it go. Now you are no longer expected
To hold in your fisted, sweat-wet hand
The reputation you have built in years
Of thoughtful care for the careless, enthusiastic bungler,
The nervous but well-meaning lover
Of everyone and all things, 'specially strays.
You can say no, now. You can step back
Your share contributed.
Can you? Or is the habit just too deep?

The Cosmic Search

Sit still, relaxed, no task or duty here.
Breathe in and out. Slowly.
More slowly than before.
Relax your hands, your fingers.
Just for now, hold nothing,
Not even a jacket-fold.
Let the cat on your knee go on sleeping.
She knows how to do this.
Like her, close your eyes.
Purr, if you can, deep down.
Begin to drift. What comes?
It will be different every single time.

Ouroboros

The end is the beginning, though no one warns you
That the circling snake will eventually catch its tail
And you will be returned to infants' total dependence
On loving care from others for every bite, drink, move.
Memories of past achievements sustained your dignity
As long as they lasted. As a bare infant, now you are again
Without teeth, clear vision, hearing that enabled you
To intercept and interpret the faintest nuance in the words
Of those around you. Everything's a blur
And you are neuter, nothing, just inert,
No strength in legs or arms or voice, and pride
Closes your teeth on pain.
The circle has been completed.
The snake has caught its tail.

Hallowe'en

On a dark night by the river
Stanley took the air
By Cookham churchyard
Just strolling, and glancing over
Ragstone walls, when he heard
A creaking, groaning, cracking
As the grass exploded,
Earth erupted, and the centuries' souls
Rose from their coffins before him
On their way to glory

He walked home stupefied.
The next morning, and the next, and the next,
He painted what he'd seen
In wonderment.

Violets

Violently, thrown across the clearing,
Indigo, in the darkling shade of dying day,
Or lilac, where the sun still thrusts itself
Lightly, weakening, into the gathering gloom
Ending the contrast that they splash against the ground.
Then, as the day dies, disappearing
Silently, closing for the night.

The Wonder Of The Moon

"Look at that picture, darling. What do you see?"
"Ooh, Daddy, it's a white plate, with grubby marks on it.
Somebody didn't do their washing up properly.
But I won't tell Mum. How far away is it, Daddy?
And if I get a wet cloth, can I give it a good clean?
Where is it really? Out there? Through the window? Oh, yes!
But that plate's broken. Did somebody drop it?
Or hit it accidentally on the edge of the table?
Half of it's missing. Where has it gone? Are the pieces
In Mr. Soames' cucumber frame? He won't like that,
Will he, Daddy? Grumpy Mr. Soames!"

Visiting The Moon

Even machines have explored only yards
From their landing. The few men who have been there
Have traversed no more than the width of a field
You might cross with your collie
On a summer afternoon. Were they bored?
No grass, no river, just the same-coloured dust
As in the next door crater, if they could get there.
No chance of a long walk, getting lost in a forest.
Why bother visiting the Moon?
Because it's there!

Interrupting Jane Austen's Maid

Yes, madam (curtsey)
Will that be all, madam (curtsey)
Now can I please go downstairs and get on, madam?
(Unsaid. No curtsey)
(Curtsey beside the door and so on out)
Now she should be comfortable enough at her desk
And I at mine for a few minutes
And I will meditate on the postboy's fair hair
And the stableboy's leg as he rises
Effortlessly into the ...
Bother the woman! There's her bell again!
Can't she give me two minutes together
To decide a word?
Up the stairs. Open the door. Curtsey.
Yes, Madam? "Philida, what's another name for..."

A Bit Of Bad Luck

It won't go away.
It has to be lived through, and
Almost certainly will be
In its own time.
If it destroys us
It will no longer matter
For we won't be here
To have to adjust
To the new ways of managing,
To buying new tools
To allow us to do
The little we can.

Angels

Because a preacher works for God
And reckoned He needed messengers,
    Do you exist?
        Does He keep you busy
        Dashing about the Universe
        Like a demented diplomat,
        Never at home to enjoy Heaven,
        Taste the ambrosia,
        Jostle in the crowds?
If we receive His answers to our prayers,
    Do they come direct,
    Like over a celestial internet?
    If so,
        Why does He or we need you?
Perhaps you are a specialist,
    Only used for particular jobs
    Like telling virgins they will bear a child
    Or tipping those capable of faith off their horses
        At a particular point on their journeys?

Do you get home-leave occasionally,
Time to rest and refresh yourself,
Polish your wings and learn the words
    For your next assignment?
Or perhaps we will discover that life after earthly death
    Is far more sophisticated than we limited humans
Can possibly imagine.

Prayer

I never understood prayer
What it is or how to do it
Fifty years of participation
Other people's words
Social rather than driven by belief

The implications of "praying to" defeat me
How can they all be right? Who said they were?
Is God a synod or a big committee?
How often are their conclusions unanimous
Or accepted in full?
So who, what answered? Anyone? Anything?
Or do we each simply work it out, or the moment passes?

Chime

In the dawn, as the sun rises, nothing moves.
The single chime is richness rising out of emptiness
Thick in its solid weight, vibrating
Through the forest, over the nearby foothills,
Round the distant peaks. It is a greeting
From the Divine to those who fear
What the new day might bring,
Surrounding them with unchanging calmness
In which to take a deep breath, confident
It may be difficult but not impossible.

Prejudice

English bred and born
And so are you, except
My parents were born in Scotland and Australia,
Yours in Kashmir.
Both our fathers drive taxis in Birmingham
Both our mothers play leading roles in our community
We went to the same school, same college
Studied the same subjects
Why do they not all realise
We are just the same?

The Ivory Bangle Lady

(Black History Month, October 2023)

Long ago – there is no way to know how long that was
But long enough for all the flesh to fall
From your bones – they buried you with honour,
Love and care in this alien land, far from your people.
No one marked your grave,
But you were held high in the respect they gave you.
They marked this with the jewels and ivory bangles
Left upon your body.

This land has always been a sanctuary
Sought by the oppressed. Sometimes the ignorant
Fail in compassion, but mostly
The heartless are defeated. Decency reigns.

Baroness Doreen Thomas

(Black History Month, October 2023)

When your son dies, stabbed casually
By boys who can find nothing better to do that day,
You weep. Your heart is broken.
How can you go on living in this world?
Is there no alternative? Are we, because we're black,
To get no justice? Must we give up?
Is that all we're worth?

No, it is not! Shame on his murderers,
And on the excusers who would rather drink their tea
Than seek out those who killed your son
And left him, hiding, terrified, to die.

Fight! Fight! With words, not violence.
And so you did. Succeeded, at least temporarily,
And gained exemplar place among the great,
Honoured, a beacon, showing us all the way.

Alma Woodsey Thomas

(Black History Month, October 2023)

Dear Alma! Brought from the oppression of Georgia Crackers
To a more tolerant North, received and gave
The joy of exuberant colour to her students
For thirty-five years, before being recognised
Aged sixty-six, What a wait, but
What a flowering into greatness! Her colours radiate
Like an atomic pile from her canvas!
The greatest admired, demanded, lived
With her inspiration and, throughout it all,
She smiled proudly, but always humble,
Knowing she had shown the way to the top
To every black child who thought they could only dream.

Names And Heritage

We hadn't a lot of which to be proud
In the grubby industrial city in which I grew up.
I was set apart by my red hair,
Bullied, the only one in my school.
It came through aunts on both sides.
What could I do?
I was told to be proud of my names,
All three an inheritance through four generations,
One that of an honoured Highland regiment,
Now merged.
One too long for some to pronounce.
Mother's father was Irish, but left little in me
Except the faeries, imagination and stories
That everyone notices but no one can really see.
Names are a heritage that history lays on us.
We have to fashion them to the society
In which we live our lives,
Abbreviating, accepting nick-names,
Adopting new ones.
What name would I choose if I could choose one just for me?

Spring Planning

Chaucer began it.
As the snow retreats
Falls from the gutters
Descends in gobbets
From the roofs
Runs in streams
Over pavements
And fills potholes
Thoughts precede the sun.
Where shall I go this summer?
Somewhere exotic
Off the brochures
Off beaten tracks
Of 'planes or even trains
To the silence of being totally alone

Lambs In Spring

First time out from the barn
They quiver against their mother's side
Before diving behind her back leg
For the comfort of the teat
Until she's had enough
And nudges them away
To learn the world.
He is suspicious
Stays close
Peers round
Until
A neighbour looks at him
Approaches
Leaps
And turns to but his mother.
Head the cheeky so-and-so off
Baaaa once, and turn to examine
This green stuff by his feet
Nose tickling
Maybe good to eat.

Spring Cinquaine

Shepherd
Capped, hunched,
Still-standing, frozen.
Dogs pant, tongues lolling.
Guardian

Paris

Wherever I travelled, I just had to go
Through Paris, staying somewhere cheap
With a breakfast bistro in the entrance hall,
Hot croissants on the counter and hard boiled eggs,
Strong coffee and Gitanes' smoke,
And later the girls from the neighbouring hotels
Would prop up the doorways, cock up legs and eyes
For the flics and the taxi drivers. Old buses
With platforms and wigwags to signal unnoticed
Intentions to turn or to stop, and the tour-boats
Needling lazily past the burnt cathedral.
A birthday cake standing above on the hill.

Night Journey

Leaving the town, he walked into the darkness.
From where the light presented everything
And gave him nothing helpful,
He plods, weighed down by nothing
Into dark nothingness, and would go on
Until fatigue dropped him
Into its gifted bed beside the fortuitous path,
And he could sleep,
Giving up the problem of where he was going
To all that was around him unseen.

Climate Change At Kandersteg

Is the glacier still there?
Has it melted quite away?
Is its face still blue as sea.
Its surface soot-scattered and crevassed?
And the melt-stream at its foot,
Is it still as clear and pure,
Running through the clattering fan
Of outwashed pebbles at its foot,
Round as bullets in the sun?

Kittiwakes

Kittiwakes, where have you been?
At last you're back on your ledges
Sweeping and diving around your familiar waves
This year.
But next year? In ten years' time?
They say the ocean's warming.
How sensitive are you to its warmth?
Does that mean that, next year,
More of you will abandon this cliff
And summer-settle further north or east
Beyond our tropicalizing ken?
We will miss you, friends.

Family And Friends

If I were to arrange a garden party,
Who would I invite? There wouldn't be many
And, not knowing each other,
Some would find an excuse
Or, coming duteously, would grow bored
And leave early.
We've never all sat round together
Friends and family. My social group is not integrated,
But one or two are special.
I so much value their gifts to me, and to others,
Admire how they live, relax,
Bedding down in their canal barge bunk
Or setting their tent on a narrow mountain ridge.
Most of them I met by chance, in passing.
We happened to be in the same room, same field.
Some passed through quickly, "living such busy lives",
In contrast to the care home staff who surround me daily
Whose families I know from all their stories
Told as they lovingly shower me, and carefully make my bed.
Polyglot. Separate. What is left after a lifetime of wandering,
Finding and losing people on the way?

Claw Wisdom

You sit on my knees immobile
Exercising your unsheathed claws
In my pain
But I don't move. I couldn't
Because it is your choice, your pleasure.
You sit purring for minutes
Clearly thinking,
Contemplating all the wisdom
That you and your forecats have accumulated
During all the hours
You sat immobile
On other people's knees.

Communication

Suppose Mr. Tibbs could speak.
But does he need to? Does his waving tail,
His wide-spread whiskers,
His carefully-placed, one-in-front-of-the-other, feet,
Not tell me exactly what he has noticed,
What he fears, or what's amusing him?
What he wants is reflected
In the intensity of his stare,
A long stroke down his back,
A scratch on the top of his skull between his ears,
Food – often food, splashed in his empty plate.
Mr. Tibbs dominates any room he enters, silently.
What more could he have to say?

Curiosity

We are curious, which nearly killed my cat
Gizzy, many times. She is a beautiful tabby, half-Siamese,
With pointed ears and a piercing miaow
When not being silent, dignified, alone.
Inveterably curious, used to getting closed
In neighbours' sheds, or disappearing
For days, returning thinner and ready to eat a horse,
With her character slightly altered by
All her new untold experiences.
So it used to be with me, when I could,
But I am wearing out and missing travel
To places where peoples' context is different,
A new language to learn, peculiar shops,
Strange street-smells and architecture,
But the same kind hospitality everywhere to save me
As it saves my cat on her secret travels, too.

Why Do Cats Exist?

Why do cats exist?
To teach humans not to rush about continually,
To explain the value of lying still
    In a bed, or bath or carpet
    Just watching, meditation,
    Letting the world digest itself,
        And, in the resulting calm,
            Accept, move on.

Why do cats exist?
To offer the comfort of having
Someone to stroke when no one else is there,
Saying nothing audible, moving not at all
Unless a leg or whisker needs adjustment
To put it back immaculate from where
A careless hand disturbed it into irregularity.

Why do cats exist?
To warn we humans with a paw, a meow,
A look, a rush and jump, of dangers,
      Unexpected visitors,
      Things falling,
Butterflies we haven't seen,
      Saviours of our insufficient selves.

Bobbled

What is this thing in my bed?
I leap in, and someone's left this
THING on my blanket, woolly and soft
But *BOBBLED*, hugely bobbled
All over it, like giant pustules,
Bright *ORANGE*,
Even round the edge.
It can't stay here.
I'll hook its brim.
Oh, now it's caught in my claw as I jerk it,
And it falls back,
And its bobbles won't let me roll it onto the floor.
At last. When I get down
I'll roll it under the sofa.
Whose bed is this anyway?

Introduction

She nuzzled her son
As if showing him off to me,
Comforting him in his insecurity
At seeing such a strange creature
Upright on two legs.
He whiffled as I offered
The back of my hand
To his nostrils, and they widened
As he sniffed, then uneasily
Shuffled his vulnerable legs.
His mother watched,
Confident, caring,
Blowing gently on the top of his head.
He would know this odd thing –
Man – next time he met him
And know not to be afraid.

Worker Bee

Sitting beside the lavender hedge
She visited me, buzzing gently and humbly,
To test several blossoms
Until she found one ready to give up its goodness.

She paused there, packing her pouches,
Looked at me, almost nodded "Good morning",
And took off for her hive, carrying
Back home her precious load for the winter.

Had we met before when she was searching my garden?
Had she been directed here by colleagues' dancing?
Had she floated past my nose while I sat somnolently
Doing nothing in contrast to her purposefulness?

Would I have recognised her among her comrades?
Doubtful, though perhaps she recognised me.

Euphoria I

Her name is Eloise. She lays her ears neatly along her back,
Tucks her legs beneath her into the long damp grass,
Sniffs the air, nose wrinkling, in eager interest
At the smells the early morning breeze brings to the garden.
Lifts her head. In sight there is a row of lettuce,
Pale green, succulent, moist with remaining dew,
Which she will visit soon without fear of recrimination.
She has nibbled there before and will again
But now she enjoys the joy of knowing
She is loved and will be cared for
Among the dandelions, warm in the summer sun.

Euphoria II

Phillip is browny-green, with big flattish eyes,
A scaly skin that camouflages him
Against the surface of the fallen branch
Conveniently stretching across the mud into the lake.
It hides him from the gangly, sharp-eyed heron
Who isn't here yet, but doubtless will glide past,
Hunting, when the golden evening comes.
Now and then, a fly will float lazily past Phillip's nose
And his tongue may uncurl sharply to warn it
That it would be taken if the sun were not so warm
And he wasn't quite so comfortable and content.

Red Leather Slippers

I didn't need new slippers, but
There in the shop I simply couldn't resist them.
I was looking for holiday sandals, plain, brown, strappy,
And the flash of the slippers' crimson caught the corner of my eye.
"Ah," I said out loud, and I seldom talk to myself in shops,
But I couldn't help it. Love does that to you,
And I loved them, had to bring them home.
If only I could walk down the street in them,
Let them flash at the neighbours
As I glide gracefully by.

Disaster Barely Averted

It was all arranged. Celebrant briefed, quiet hymns and poems chosen,
Relatives and friends invited, new black suits, white shirts and blouses bought,
And the last three suitable hats available locally.
The service was to be at ten, and crematorium staff are always nearly overwhelmed
By the pressure of time and the next family behind.
At half-past eight, the undertaker 'phoned:
"The hearse won't start; I can't get grandpa to you."
"It has to go on," we said. "Everyone will be on their way already."
"It can't," he said, "not without Grandpa."

Outside, Selena's horsebox drew up.
"Can't stay for the wake," she said, "I'm jumping Sinbad in Colchester at two."
"Don't worry," we told the undertaker, "We've got transport.
Just get him in his box, all nice and tidy.
We'll pick him up in half an hour."

Unavoidable Family Christmas

Everyone called together, everyone comes.
Even Big Willie the Bully
Whose kids keep quiet, and whose wife
Still shows the signs of their last disagreement
Around the edges of her carefully made-up face.
And Joey the Joker still making silly jokes
Which only he laughs at, and Paula,
Trying to shush him, unsuccessfully.
And Grandpa, napkin in his collar,
Gravy-stained from the start.
But what really finishes me off after lunch is
The interminable games they all want to play
That I've never heard of, and nobody explains.

He Wasn't There Again Today

The doorbell rings. I struggle to the wheelchair,
Switch on, wait for contact, push the joystick forward
Turn into the hall lined with bookshelves.
Every shelf is full, books standing, lying sideways
Waiting to be read or collected by a sensitive visitor,
Interspersed with china cats and
A big green vase with earrings on each side.
On the opposite wall, my pictures
From when I fancied myself an artist,
A fjord, a Scots valley, an illustration
For a short story from many years ago.
Round the right-angled corner, two cupboards,
Doors neatly closed, but the lights inside
Come on when the doors are opened.
And there I am at the front door.
Open it – and there's no-one there.
Just a parcel blocking my exit
Too heavy, shiny, smooth,
To be lifted from my chair without assistance
But the deliveryman gave up waiting
While I was touring my hall.

I Will Smile

(after Carole Satyamurti)

When I hand the last leaking milk carton to the shop assistant

When I suggest to my neighbour that he parks his car more tidily

When next door's poodle scrapes her paws down my clean trousers

When Mother-in-law drops in for tea

When I splash paint indelibly on my best shirt

When Councillor Jones calls to canvas my vote

When my credit card is refused again

When Gwen tips over her full teacup, waving her hands in enthusiasm

When I lose at darts, bridge, golf, snakes and ladders...

Whenever life turns irredeemably against me, I WILL smile.

Index of Titles

A Bit Of Bad Luck 65
Acknowledgements 5
Across Vauxhall Bridge 17
A Doorway In Granada 26
A Feather 25
Alma Woodsey Thomas 73
Almost 21
Angels 66
An Unsure Hand 47
Apple Green 13
A Thousand Tiny Collisions 29
At The Fold In The Map 19
Autumn 39
Autumn Of Love 34
Baroness Doreen Thomas 72
Bear Kindness 28
Bobbled 87
Boxfiles 55
Broken Isolation 22
Caress 24
Changes 38
Chime 69
Claw Wisdom 83
Climate Change At Kandersteg 80
Coin 16
Communication 84
Curiosity 85
Dignity 46
Disabled Visitors 48
Disaster Barely Averted 93
Early Lesson 15
Euphoria I 90

Euphoria II	91
Family And Friends	82
Flying A Glider	42
Friday	41
Hallowe'en	60
He Wasn't There Again Today	95
Holding Hands	23
I Am	36
Interrupting Jane Austen's Maid	64
Introduction	88
Invocation	50
I Will Smile	96
Kittiwakes	81
Lambs In Spring	76
Layers	37
Let It Go	57
Letter From Love	30
Names And Heritage	74
Night Journey	79
October	40
Ouroboros	59
Paris	78
Pedantry	35
Prayer	68
Prejudice	70
Red Leather Slippers	92
Reply To Love's Letter	31
Return	32
Salvation	56
Season's End, Hastings	43
Snow Gulley	45
Somelier	20
Sporting Preference	18
Spring Cinquaine	77
Spring Planning	75

Survival	44
The Cosmic Search	58
The Ivory Bangle Lady	71
The Kitchen Range	14
The Last Five Years	52
The Table	54
The Wonder Of The Moon	62
Two Couples	49
Unavoidable Family Christmas	94
Violets	61
Visiting The Moon	63
What Would I Do Without You?	51
Why Do Cats Exist?	86
Worker Bee	89

Index Of First Lines

A black bear came through my kitchen door. 28
Always so much to remember. 40
Among the demanding icons on my desktop, ... 24
Atoms buzz silently in my bloodstream, ... 29
Because a preacher works for God 66
Chaucer began it. 75
Clamour can be so demanding 22
Dear … 30
Dear Alma! Brought from the oppression
of Georgia Crackers 73
Dear Love. 31
English bred and born 70
Even machines have explored only yards 63
Everyone called together, everyone comes. 94
exhausted by trying to do more
than my body approves of 36
First thing in a morning,
once I've been washed and dressed 51
First time out from the barn 76
Flying a glider isn't difficult. 42
Friday, I leave it all behind, ... 41
From the bow, watching the ice wall approach, ... 44
Heavy air, thick, too difficult to breathe 32
Her name is Eloise.
She lays her ears neatly along her back 90
I am 35
I didn't need new slippers, but 92
I do have a table, with a generous surface area 54
If I were a coin 16
If I were to arrange a garden party, ... 82
I never understood prayer 68
In the cobbled street across the valley 26

In the darkness underneath the bed 50
In the dark, our hands touched 23
In the dawn, as the sun rises, nothing moves. 69
I sat at the end on the left, ... 15
Is the glacier still there? 80
It was all arranged. Celebrant briefed,
quiet hymns and poems chosen, ... 93
It won't go away. 65
Kittiwakes, where have you been? 81
Leaving the town, he walked into the darkness. 79
Let It go. You haven't been allowed in years to 57
"Let's visit the Castle", everyone said 48
Long ago – there is no way to know how long that was 71
Long, dun, soft as silk, ... 25
"Look at that picture, darling. What do you see?" 62
Not everything changes, over however long. 38
Nothing stands still, even when 37
Not in your face, your lips, your eyes, ... 34
Now it's September. Everyone has gone home 39
Oh, the temptation! She sat low in the water. 21
On a dark night by the river 60
One way, we cycled into the hard East wind 19
Phillip is browny-green, with big flattish eyes, ... 91
Red Routemasters clustered in Camberwell Green 17
Returning from the helpful optometrist 46
Set into the wall, and forbidden 14
She nuzzled her son 88
Shepherd 77
Sit still, relaxed, no task or duty here. 58
Sitting beside the lavender hedge 89
Space beneath my feet. It should be snow. 45
Suppose Mr. Tibbs could speak. 84
Tennis in the park on a hot Wednesday. 18
Ten years ago, there were two of us. 52
The doorbell rings. I struggle to the wheelchair, ... 95
The end is the beginning, though no one warns you 59

The light in here isn't good.	47
There have been two Autumn storms already	43
The smell hits you as you climb the unsteady ladder	13
The stick was hanging on the arm of the bench	49
Violently, thrown across the clearing,	61
We are curious, which nearly killed my cat	85
We hadn't a lot of which to be proud	74
What is this thing in my bed?	87
"What shall we drink with this, everybody?	20
When I hand the last leaking milk carton to the shop assistant	96
When your son dies, stabbed casually	72
Wherever I travelled, I just had to go	78
Whirling, whirling, whirling	56
Why did I choose the red boxfiles	55
Why do cats exist?	86
Yes, madam (curtsey)	64
You sit on my knees immobile	83

novum PUBLISHER FOR NEW AUTHORS

Rate this book on our website!

www.novum-publishing.co.uk

The author

After a diverse and fulfilling career as an academic, civil servant, and international management consultant, retirement allowed Robert Ferguson to rediscover his early passion for imaginative writing, a pursuit he had loved since childhood.

Finding himself in the West Midlands of England, he discovered a rich and dynamic literary culture that inspired him to immerse himself in writing and publishing. His work spans short stories, poetry, reviews, and a novel, each reflecting his sharp insights and storytelling skill. Over time, his efforts earned recognition, with his pieces frequently published and occasionally winning awards for their originality and depth.

For Robert, retirement has become a deeply rewarding chapter, where the joy of storytelling shapes his days. A lifetime traveller, Robert draws on rich memories of places, people and animals – especially cats! – to reflect the world for which he retains a deep and passionate love.

novum PUBLISHER FOR NEW AUTHORS

The publisher

*He who stops
getting better
stops being good.*

This is the motto of novum publishing, and our focus is on finding new manuscripts, publishing them and offering long-term support to the authors.
Our publishing house was founded in 1997, and since then it has become THE expert for new authors and has won numerous awards.

Our editorial team will peruse each manuscript within a few weeks free of charge and without obligation.

You will find more information about
novum publishing and our books on the internet:

w w w . n o v u m - p u b l i s h i n g . c o . u k

Robert Ferguson

Start to Finish

ISBN 978-3-99131-754-8
74 pages

Wander through your life; the seasons, months, weather, national events, and personal pleasures. Sit with these poems, remember, and enjoy.

Robert Ferguson
Love and Other Thoughts

ISBN 978-3-99131-907-8
78 pages

Love comes at every stage in life, and always surprises us, not always happily, but always with a lasting bite.

Robert Ferguson
Everyone On My Street

ISBN 978-3-99146-490-7
84 pages

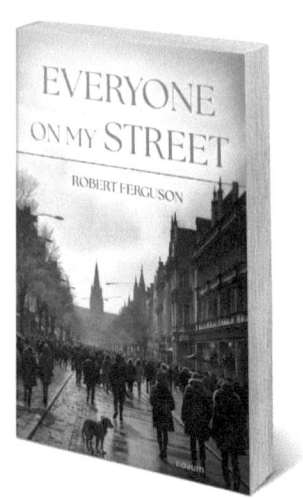

Diverse Britain! What an opportunity to learn about other people's values, fears, difficulties, ambitions, and fulfilments! Just look around your street. "Everyone On My Street" is a series of poems that tells the stories of all of these different people.